Weird
Sports Day

There are lots of Early Reader stories you might enjoy.

Look at the back of the book or, for a complete list, visit www.orionbooks.co.uk

Weird
Sports Day

By Alan, Rachel
and Megan Gibbons

Illustrated by
Jane Porter

Orion
Children's Books

First published in Great Britain in 2015
by Orion Children's Books
an imprint of Hachette Children's Group
and published by Hodder & Stoughton
Orion House
5 Upper Saint Martin's Lane
London WC2H 9EA
An Hachette UK Company

1 3 5 7 9 10 8 6 4 2

Text © Alan Gibbons, Rachel Gibbons and Megan Gibbons 2015
Illustrations © Jane Porter 2015

The moral right of Alan Gibbons, Rachel Gibbons
and Megan Gibbons and Jane Porter to be identified as
authors and illustrator of this work has been asserted.

The paper and board used in this paperback are natural and recyclable
products made from wood grown in sustainable forests.
The manufacturing processes conform to the environmental
regulations of the country of origin.

ISBN 978 1 4440 1280 4

A catalogue record for this book is available from the British Library.

Printed and bound in China

www.orionchildrensbooks.co.uk

To all at
Garston C of E Primary School

Contents

One

It's weird being a Weirdibeast.
Look at Katie Cat. She isn't just
a cat. She is half-owl.

She is a Miaowl. All of her friends are a funny mix of things too.

One Monday morning, Katie's teacher, Mrs Creature had some very exciting news.

"We are going to take part in an Animal Sports Day," she said.

"Let's try on our new sports kits. We need to see if they fit."

But there were all sorts of problems.
Ricky Rabbit put his sports kit on.
His legs popped out all over
the place.

He tumbled backwards and lay
on his back.
"I've got eight legs," he grumbled.
"And only two leg holes."

Dabby Dog tried his on. The spikes poked through and tore his shirt.

"Oh!" he moaned.

Katie Cat and Tony Pony tried theirs on. Their wings kept popping out.

"Oh!" they groaned.

Penny Pig pulled on her shorts.
Her old curly, whirly tail used to fit,
but not her big, bushy squirrel tail.
It ripped the back of the shorts.

"Oh no!" said all her friends.

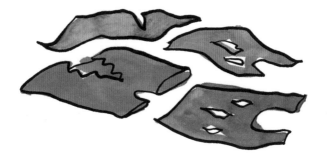

Two

Mrs Creature counted:
"One, two, three, four, five.

Uh oh."

"What's wrong?" the Weirdibeasts asked.
"We need six to make a team," Mrs Creature growled.

"I know," Katie Cat said. "We can get somebody from the other class. What about Ellie the Elephant."

"Cool," everybody cried. "She will be so big and strong."

Mrs Creature sent for Ellie.
The door swung open and . . .

. . . nobody walked in!
"Where is she?" Penny asked.

"I'm down here," came a tiny voice.

They looked down and saw a teeny-weeny, grey animal. She had the trunk and tusks of an elephant and the ears, paws, whiskers and tail of a mouse.

"I'm not just an elephant anymore," she squeaked. "I'm an Ellie-Mouse."

The other animals barked and neighed and oinked and snapped and too-wit-too-wooed. "Hello Ellie-Mouse," they said.

Suddenly Ellie screamed. She had seen her reflection in the window.

What's wrong?" Katie Cat asked
as Ellie trembled behind a chair.
Mrs Creature shook her head.
"Didn't you know, children?
Elephants are scared of mice."

Penny Pig shook her head. "I don't think we're going to win at this Sports Day."

Three

On the morning of the Sports
Day all the schools were there.

First to arrive were the kangaroos.

Then there were the cheeky
monkeys.

Last of all, there were the
cheetahs.

When the Weirdibeasts walked in everybody stared.

"They're all mixed up!"
laughed the kangaroos.
"They're so strange,"
chattered the monkeys.
"They're weird,"
growled the cheetahs.

"Hello! We're the Weirdibeasts,"
said the Weirdibeasts.

Four

The first event was the sprint.
Everybody lined up.

"Ready, steady, go!"
The Weirdibeasts set off . . .

. . . just as the cheetahs crossed the line at the other end of the track.

"I didn't see them go," said
Katie Cat.

The second event was the long jump. When Penny Pig jumped the sand flew everywhere.

Ricky Rabbit had a go, but he
jumped sideways.

Katie Cat and Tony Pony didn't
do any better. They tried to fly.

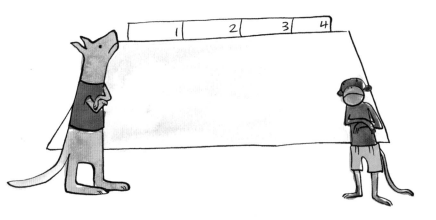

"That's cheating," said the other
animals.

Ellie the Elephant was their last hope. She jumped with all her might and vanished in the sand pit.

It took ages to find her.
"That was scary," she said.

"We're not doing very well,"
Dabby Dog said. "We've not
won anything."

Five

The next event was tree climbing.

Penny Pig was climbing high until the branch broke and she fell. "I don't think pigs belong in trees," the monkeys laughed.

The monkeys were the best at climbing.

"I don't like trees," Ellie the Elephant said. "They're scary."

Finally, it was time for the relay.
"The cheetahs are going to win,"
Katie Cat grumbled.
"They are very fast," Penny Pig
agreed.

The race started and the cheetahs
were in the lead.

The kangaroos bounded past
Penny Pig.

Tony Pony took over from Ricky.
He passed the monkey in front
of him.

Dabby Dog was next. He passed the kangaroo in front of him.

Katie Cat was last to go.
"Look," everybody said.
"The cheetah is out of puff."

Katie and the cheetah were neck
and neck.

Then the cheetah tripped Katie
Cat.

"Oh no," Penny Pig cried.

But something surprising happened.

Ellie the Elephant flew past the cheetah and over the line.

The Weirdibeasts had won!

"Where did you come from?"
they asked her.
"I was hiding on Katie Cat's
back," Ellie said. "I was scared."

Everybody cheered. The little Ellie-Mouse had won the biggest race of all.

What are you going to read next?

More adventures with Horrid Henry,

or go exploring with Shumba,

and brave the Jungle

and Arctic with Algy.

Find a frog prince with Tulsa

or even a big, yellow, whiskery

Lion in the Meadow!

Tuck into some

Blood and Guts and
Rats' Tail Pizza,

learn to dance with
Sophie,

travel back
in time with

Cudweed

and sail away in

Noah's Ark.

Enjoy all the Early Readers.